May I Have The First Dance?
By
Sonja Paschal Linsley

Lovingly dedicated to the
irrepressible father of my children
who joyfully dances with us all.

Illustrated
By
Paul Adam Linsley

"May I have the first dance?"
Daddy said with a grin,

Then he lifted his newborn,
Held her close to his chin.

And gently he swayed
In the light of the moon

'Till her cries were all quiet
And far too soon.

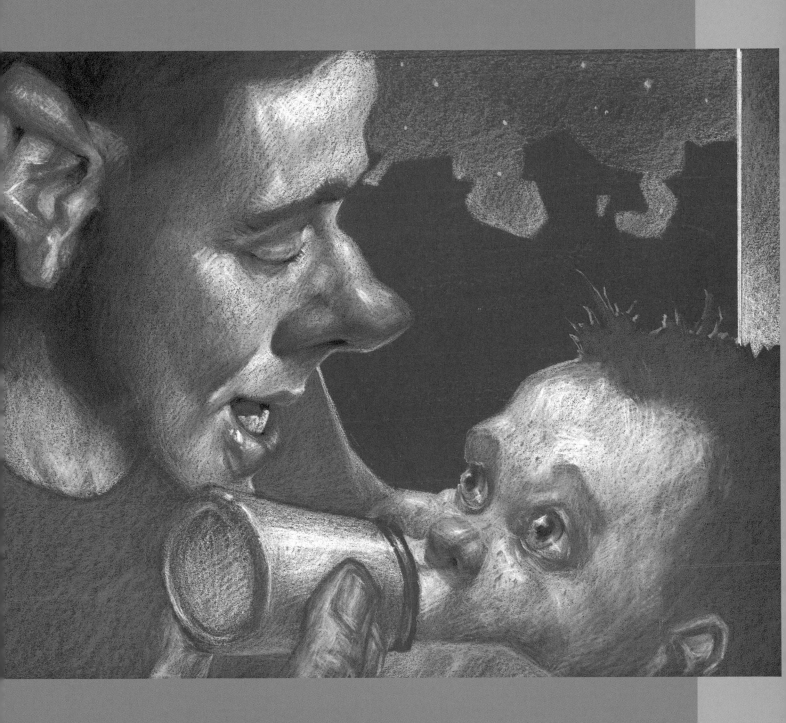

"May I have the first dance?"

Daddy said with a flair,

Then he tossed his todler

High up in the air.

And she laughed,

And she giggled,

And begged him for more

'Til they both fell exhausted

In heaps on the floor.

"May I have the first dance?"
Daddy said with repose,

Then he held his sweet girl
While she danced on his toes.

Her first day of school
Could wait just a while

For her Daddy to dance
Her fears to a smile.

"May I have the first dance?"
  Daddy said with a flair,

Then he kicked the soccer ball
  High in the air.

So she charged 'cross the field
  In a thrilling display.

And they ran
  And they laughed
    And they played
      Hard that day.

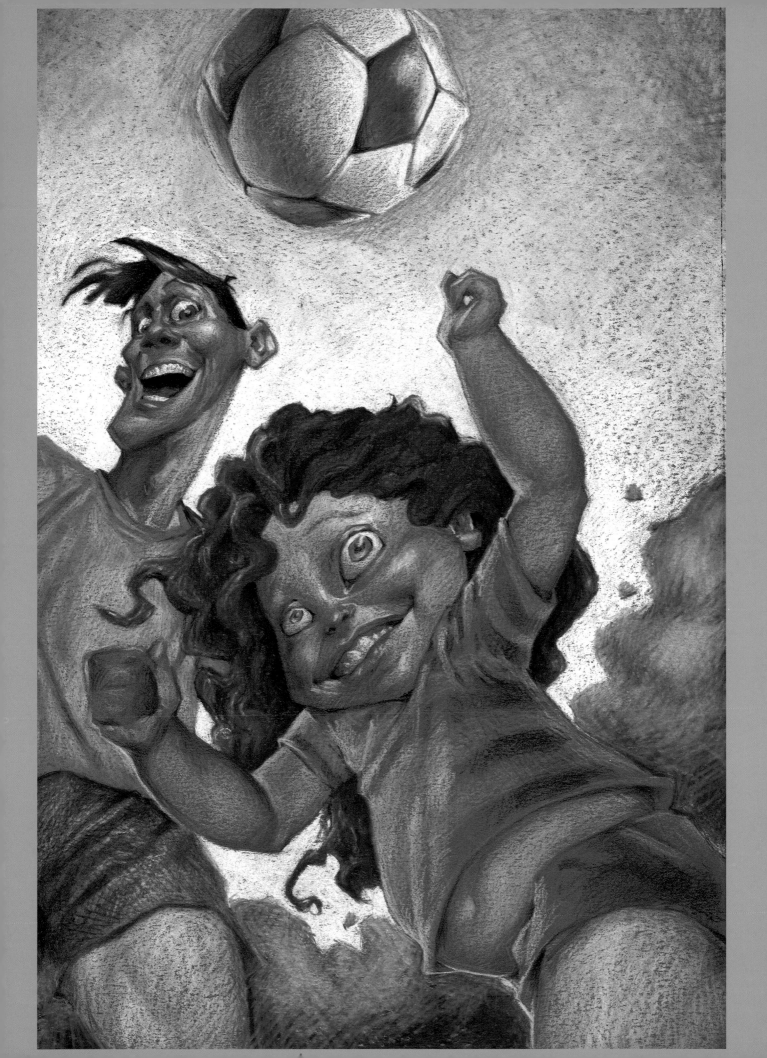

"May I have the first dance?"

Daddy said with aplomb,

As he heard

The sound of the radio on.

And he twisted and turned

Full of giggling young girls

And he joined in the twirls.

"May I have the first dance?"
Daddy tried to look past

The pained broken leg,
The crutches and cast.

Then he hugged her tight,
Spun her 'round on one leg

And never showed her
That he was afraid.

"May I have the first dance?"

Daddy hoisted a roller

And they opened the paint can

Admiring the color.

Then they taped

And they scraped,

Preparations were made

And they painted her room

In her favorite pink shade.

"May I have the first dance?"

Daddy said with a tear,

As she came down to wait

'Till her first date was here.

And he held her close

'Till the knock on the door

When he feared their dances

Would soon be no more.

"May I have the first dance?"

Daddy said with a smile,

As he waited to walk

His child down the aisle.

And he held her arm,

Then they walked that day

To the alter

And there

He gave her away.

"May I have the first dance?"

His smile was the best,

As he held his

New granddaughter

Close to his chest.

And gently he swayed

To a lullaby tune

And remembered his daughter

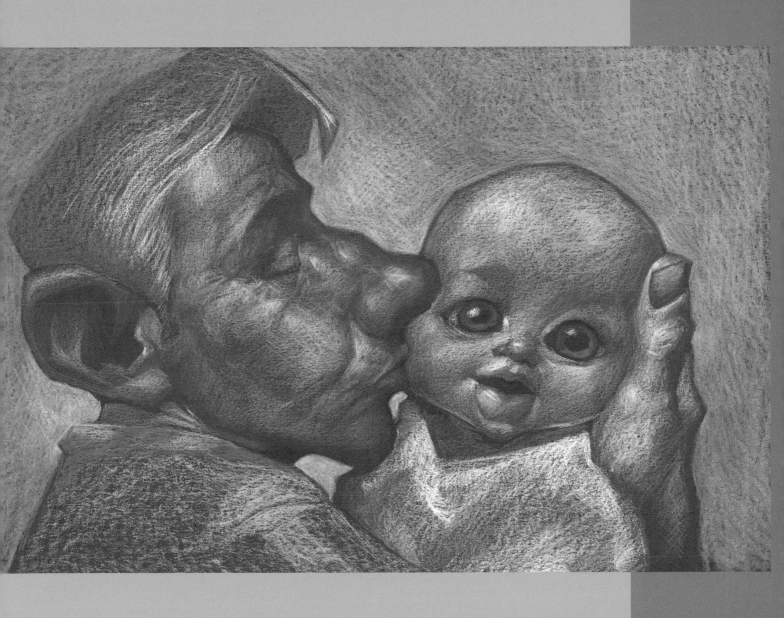

Had grown up too soon.

"May I have the first dance?"
She whispered the query

But his legs were too weak,
And his bones were too weary.

He gazed in her eyes
And there he could see

That together they'd
Dance
Through
Eternity.